Suppandi
FIRE AWAY

A painter, a driver, a copywriter, and even a chef, Suppandi has applied his truly unique wit to almost every imaginable job out there. The perpetual optimist, Suppandi is never afraid to take up a new occupation, much to the amusement of his fans everywhere. Suppandi has remained, from the day of the character's conception, *Tinkle's* most popular toon.

Based on Tamil folklore, Suppandi was first drawn by the legendary Ram Waeerkar. His daughter, Archana Amberkar, took over after he passed away. She gave the character a more youthful look. In this collection, we have put together Suppandi tales illustrated by Archana Amberkar, Savio Mascarenhas, Abhijeet Kini and Prachi Killekar. The latter has drawn several Little Suppandi episodes which showcase the childhood escapades of our hero. The adventures of the superhero avatar of Suppandi have been illustrated by Savio Mascarenhas.

Suppandi has a resume that is long enough to fill an entire book. We came up with this collection keeping that thought in mind—we hope you love it.

Only one word to say for my favourite toon, Suppandi 'Hilarious'!
- **Navamallika Sarma,** *Guwahati, Assam*

I cannot control my laugh when I read the Suppandi stories.
– **Neha Chandran,** *Chennai*

Suppandi does only one job extremely well. He makes us laugh.
– **Shanaya Phaldesai,** *Goa*

My toddler sister and my grandmother, both equally love Suppandi. He has no age-limit.
– **Sanjana Vajrapu,** *Visakhapatnam, A.P*

The way Suppandi goofs up makes me rolling on the floor with laughter. He is the best!
- **Darshana Balakrishnan,** *Chennai*

Wherever Suppandi goes, chaos ensues! Medini
– **Sundarrajan,** *Bangalore*

Suppandi is just wonderful. He is the ultimate comedy-dose.
- **Utkarsh Shukla, Bareilly,** *Uttar Pradesh*

A tinkle magazine without a Suppandi tale is like incomplete.
– **CS Janani,** *Jabalpur, Madhya Pradesh*

Under the Table...3-5

The Vanishing Magic!...6-9

Princess Soupy...10-14

Tyred Out!...15-17

Start, Camera, Action!..18-26

Suppandi Gives Directions...27-28

Once When Suppandi Was Young: Saving Time.........29

Meet Chiyo and SuperWeirdos......................................30

Chiyo: Twice the Trouble..31-38

SuperWeirdos: Boom!...40-46

Super Suppandi and the Mutant Mouse......................47-56

Suppandi, The Miner...57-59

The Rat Bait...60-63

Goal!...64-66

Hot and Cold...67-68

Hand Signal...69-70

ONE DAY, SUPPANDI'S EMPLOYER GETS A VISIT FROM INCOME TAX OFFICERS—

COME IN, COME IN, I WAS EXPECTING YOU!

KNOCK KNOCK

UNDER THE TABLE

WRITER: PRASAD IYER

ART: ARCHANA AMBERKAR

COLOUR: SHAILEE

PEOPLE ARE JEALOUS OF MY SUCCESS. THEY SAY I MADE MONEY THROUGH ILLEGAL MEANS. THEY SAY I HAVE A LOT OF BLACK MONEY...

...BUT IT IS NOT SO. I'M TOTALLY INNOCENT OF ALL THESE CHARGES.

WE'RE JUST HERE ON ROUTINE INSPECTION, SIR.

4

5

THE VANISHING MAGIC!

WRITER: ANISHA HARIHARAN	ART: ARCHANA AMBERKAR	COLOUR: ADARSH ACHARI

SUPPANDI WAS WINDOW-SHOPPING IN A POSH MALL—

HMM... WISH I COULD AFFORD TO BUY ONE OF THESE T-SHIRTS...BUT WHAT'S THE USE?

I DON'T EVEN HAVE A TENNER IN MY POCKET!

HEY... ISN'T THAT ZORBO ZOLDERMO, THE FAMOUS MAGICIAN?

HE'S PERFORMING HERE... AND... AND... OH, WOW!

TONIGHT AT THE GREAT GALAXY THEATRE
ZORBO ZOLDERMO
ZORBO NEEDS A SKILLED ASSISTANT, INTERESTED PERSONS CAN MEET HIM AT HIS OFFICE.

HE NEEDS AN ASSISTANT!

THIS IS MY GOLDEN OPPORTUNITY TO WORK WITH A MAGICIAN!

AT ZORBO ZOLDERMO'S OFFICE—

SO, TELL ME... WHAT DO YOU KNOW ABOUT MAGIC?

DO YOU KNOW ANYTHING ABOUT VANISHING TRICKS?

OH, YES, SIR! VERY OFTEN I'VE TO VANISH FROM A PLACE AT A MOMENT'S NOTICE!..

SO HE HAS SOME EXPERIENCE... NOT AS DUMB AS HE LOOKS!

HOW UNCLE LARRY'S FRIEND USED TO ENTERTAIN US WITH HIS MAGIC TRICKS... I WISH I KNEW HOW HE PERFORMED THEM!

WELL, I'M APPOINTING YOU AS THE STAGE MANAGER. IT'LL BE YOUR RESPONSIBILITY TO SET THE STAGE BEFORE EACH PERFORMANCE.

YES, MR. ZORBO!

I AM A **PERFECTIONIST**, SUPPANDI! EVERYTHING THAT YOU DO SHOULD BE **PERFECT**! UNDERSTAND?

OF COURSE, MR. ZORBO!

SWEEP THOSE CORNERS... DUST THOSE BANNERS, NOT A SPECK OF DIRT SHOULD BE THERE!

HEY, THERE'S A LOOSE BOARD HERE!

HOW CARELESS CAN PEOPLE GET!

SUPPANDI! SUPPANDI!

COMING, MR. ZORBO!

SOMETIME LATER, THE MAGIC SHOW BEGAN. THE AUDIENCE WAS ENTHRALLED—

TADAAH!

CLAP! CLAP!

CLAP! CLAP!

THE SHOW PROCEEDED BRILLIANTLY. SOON—

AND NOW, FOR THE GRAND FINALE, 'THE VANISHING BEAUTY!'

MAGIC HERE, MAGIC THERE; MAKE THIS BEAUTY DISAPPEAR!

BEHOLD! SHE HAS...

BOO! BOO!

BOO! BOO!

WHAT ARE YOU STILL DOING HERE?

SIR, THE TRAP WOULDN'T OPEN!

AND NO WONDER!

YES, THE FLOORBOARD WAS LOOSE HERE, MR. ZORBO. BEING A PERFECTIONIST MYSELF...

...I NAILED IT SHUT

AND OF COURSE, SUPPANDI NAILED HIS CAREER IN MAGIC SHUT TOO!

9

14

STORY: SAVIO A. MASCARENHAS
SCRIPT: ANVITA SUDARSHAN
ART: ARCHANA AMBERKAR

TYRED OUT!

TRALALAA... HMM... HMM

OH OH! LOOKS LIKE WE HAVE SOME PROBLEM HERE!

THE FRONT RIGHT TYRE HAS LESS AIR. WE'LL HAVE TO STOP AT THE NEAREST PETROL PUMP TO FILL AIR.

YES, UNCLE LARRY.

* HINDI FOR ROADSIDE EATERY

START, CAMERA, ACTION!

WRITER: ANISHA HARIHARAN

ART: ARCHANA AMBERKAR

COLOUR: UMESH SARODE

LOOK! IT'S SUNDER!

I WONDER IF GOGA MASTER IS HERE...HE'S MY FAVOURITE ACTOR!!

YOU REMEMBER HIS FAMOUS ROLE AS A VILLAIN...

OF COURSE!!

NOBODY INSULTS GOGA MASTER...TAKE THIS AND...THIS...!!!

OWW! SUPPANDI!! WATCH OUT!!

MEANWHILE, THERE WAS A CRISIS HAPPENING AT THE FILM SETS–

MANOJ KAPOOR IS DOWN WITH FLU! HE CAN'T COME...!

WE HAVE TO FINISH THIS SCENE TODAY! FIND A SUBSTITUTE!

FORTUNATELY IT'S A SMALL ROLE... PICK SOMEBODY FROM THAT CROWD OF ONLOOKERS!

ERRR... OKAY!

YES! DIDN'T YOU SEE THEIR PHOTOS IN TODAY'S NEWSPAPER?

OH YES! I REMEMBER THE HEADLINES TOO, "RANGA PANGA BREAK OUT OF PRISON!!"

COINCIDENTALLY, RANGA AND PANGA ARE ALSO PRESENT THERE—

SO MANY PEOPLE... SO MANY POCKETS!!

YES, WE COULD MAKE A GOOD HAUL!

LET'S GET TO WORK! TIME IS MONEY!!

THE SHOOTING BEGINS—

OKAY, EVERYONE! LET'S FINISH THIS QUICKLY!

I'M GOING TO BE THE NEW VILLAIN IN JOLLYWOOD!

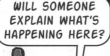

ART: PRACHI KILLEKAR

LITTLE SUPPANDI WAS IN CLASS—

ARVIND

PRESENT, TEACHER.

SOHAN

PRESENT, TEACHER.

WHY ARE YOU CALLING OUT THE NAMES, TEACHER?

TO SEE WHO IS PRESENT AND WHO IS ABSENT.

I KNOW A QUICKER WAY, TEACHER.

TELL ME, LITTLE SUPPANDI.

WHOEVER IS ABSENT PLEASE RAISE YOUR HAND.

GAK !

? ? ?

SUPPANDI & FRIENDS

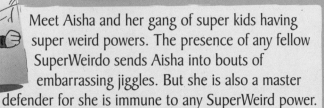

ENOUGH ABOUT ME NOW. LET'S TAKE A BREAK AND DISCOVER SOME OF THE OTHER STARS OF THE TINKLE WORLD.

Meet Aisha and her gang of super kids having super weird powers. The presence of any fellow SuperWeirdo sends Aisha into bouts of embarrassing jiggles. But she is also a master defender for she is immune to any SuperWeird power. She can also create a protective shield around herself. With such an impressive arsenal, I am sure she can become a formidable football player. But being a defender is not enough for her, she wants to become a striker! Every now and then, she embarks on a quest to gain a 'real' superpower. And in her quest, she discovers other kids who are only weirder than her. Take Rohan for instance. He can channel electricity through his body and zap people if need be. I am sure he doesn't have to worry about paying his electricity bills. But with great powers, comes great problems, the biggest being Aisha's arch-enemy Zeck. He doesn't have any superpowers but he never fails to create a super-mess. He wants to make the world laugh, whether it wants to or not. Well, an easier way to do it would be tell them some of the reasons I got fired over. So, turn the page and join this super-duper gang as they save the day, in their own weird way of course.

Chiyo might seem like a delicate teenage girl, but don't mistake her cuteness for weakness. This half-Indian, half-Japanese girl is a trained Samurai warrior and spends her spare time straightening all those loopy bad guys. Her martial arts teacher, Yamabushi makes sure that her skills stay as sharp as a katana. Huh? Does it mean that he is a human whetstone? Anyway, Chiyo is a bit short-tempered but her best friend, Geeta always cools her down, just like Maddy helps my employers cool down. Her partner in crime, or should I say crime-fighting, is Umar. He is a martial artist himself and always has Chiyo's back.

Going about her daily life, Chyo often encounters messy situations. Using her martial art skills, she gives the goons a taste of their own medicine. The only opponents against whom she cannot win are her school books. There-there, Chiyo, we have all been there, especially I. So what are you waiting for? Turn the page and join Chiyo in an action-packed adventure. Hiyyyaah!

ChiYO: TWICE THE TROUBLE

Writer
Shriya Ghate

Pencils & Inks
Ghanshyam Bochgeri

Colours
Raghavendra Kamath

Letters
Prasad Sawant

33

37

SuperWeirdos Boom!

Story
Nachiketa S. R.

Script
Rajani Thindiath

Art
Abhijeet Kini

Letters
Prasad Sawant

SOME GET-TOGETHER OF SUPERWEIRDOS THIS! ALL USELESS WEIRDOS. EXCEPT ME! YOU KNOW? THIS GROUP NEEDS TO BE *ELECTRIFIED!*

NO, ROHAN!

Tring Tring!

HELLO?

IF YOU DON'T WANT YOUR CITY BLOWN TO SMITHEREENS, COME TO THE SILENT MEADOWS. HYUK-HYUK!

INFORM NO ONE.

GUYS, I-I HAVE TO GO SOMEWHERE. I'LL BE BACK.

WHAT'S WITH HER, HEER? WEIRDO!

SHUT UP, ROHAN! SOMETHING'S UP.

ZECK! BUT YOU WERE TAKEN AWAY TO—

—THE MENTAL ASYLUM? THANKS TO YOU AND YOUR WEIRD FRIENDS!

THAT DAY, YOU SAVED THE CITY FROM MY TICKLING MISSILES. BUT NOT THIS TIME.

THIS TIME, LET'S SEE YOU SAVE THE CITY FROM **ME!** THEY WILL ALL LAUGH AT MY COMMAND*! HYUK-HYUK!

YOU AND WHAT ARMY?

*A FAILED STAND-UP COMEDIAN, ZECK'S MISSION IN LIFE IS TO FORCE PEOPLE TO LAUGH

*Heer: SW Power: With a rub of her heel, her targets are swept backward

*Sid: SW Power: One whack and he can turn even a ball of cotton into a crazy missile

45

SUPER SUPPANDI AND THE MUTANT MOUSE

WRITER: ANISHA HARIHARAN

ART: SAVIO MASCARENHAS

COLOUR: SHAILEE

48

49

52

54

DID YOU GET THE JOB?

NO.

THE INTERVIEWER IS VERY CLEVER. HE TRAPPED ME INTO ADMITTING THAT I HAVE NEVER DUG MORE THAN 10 FEET. APPARENTLY MINES ARE MUCH DEEPER THAN THAT!

HA! HE WON'T TRAP ME SO EASILY!

SO, HAVE YOU EVER MINED? WE WANT ONLY EXPERIENCED PEOPLE.

OF COURSE, SIR! DONE IT FOR YEARS! I'VE WORKED IN MINES 20,000-30,000 FEET DEEP!

REALLY?? THAT'S WONDERFUL! YOU'RE HIRED!

BY THE WAY, WHAT KIND OF LIGHTS DID YOU USE AT 20,000 FEET?

NEVER NEEDED LIGHTS, SIR!

I'VE ALWAYS WORKED THE DAY SHIFT!

OF COURSE, SUPPANDI DIDN'T GET THE JOB!

*COTTAGE CHEESE

61

62

GOAL!

WRITER:
ANISHA HARIHARAN

ART & COLOUR:
ARCHANA AMBERKAR

IT WAS THE MOST EXCITING FOOTBALL MATCH EVER WITNESSED- ROHTAG NAGAR VERSUS BANU NAGAR! MADDY, THE CAPTAIN OF ROHTAG NAGAR, WAS TENSE!

THIS IS IT, TEAM! THE LAST FIVE MINUTES THAT WILL DECIDE OUR VICTORY!

IF WE DON'T LET A GOAL THROUGH, WE'VE WON!

NO BALL CAN GET PAST ME!

NEITHER TEAM HAD SCORED, BUT A DRAW WOULD TAKE ROHTAG NAGAR TO THE FINALS.

YES, WE NEED TO PLAY OUR BEST NOW! SUPPANDI...

YOU CAN DEPEND ON ME, MADDY!

DO YOUR BEST, BANU NAGAR! BUT THIS GAME IS GOING TO BE WON BY US!

A BANU NAGAR PLAYER GOT THE BALL...

...AND HE HAD A CLEAR SHOT AT THE GOAL...

IT WAS A TENSE MOMENT...

I HOPE SUPPANDI CAN SAVE THE GOAL!

KICK!

69

VERY GOOD, SUPPANDI! NOW KEEP GOING STRAIGHT UNTIL WE REACH HOME!

HEY!

WATCH OUT!

WHAT HAPPENED, SUPPANDI? WHY DID YOU LET GO OF THE HANDLEBARS?

WE WERE GOING STRAIGHT, SO I HELD OUT MY HANDS TO INDICATE THE DIRECTION.